Way Home

Dedicated to the largely unsung, mostly unseen workers
for young people in need — L.H.
For Geordie — G.R.

Text copyright © Libby Hathorn 1994
Illustrations copyright © Gregory Rogers 1994.

The rights of Libby Hathorn and Gregory Rogers to be identified as the author
and illustrator of this work have been asserted by them in accordance with
the Copyright, Designs and Patents Act, 1988.

Published in Great Britain in 1994 by Andersen Press,
20 Vauxhall Bridge Road, London, SWIV 2SA.

First published in 1994 as a Mark Macleod book by Random House Australia.
20 Alfred Street, Milsons Point, NSW 2061.

All rights reserved.

British Library Cataloguing in Publication Data available

ISBN 0 86264 541 7

Gregory Rogers used charcoal and pastel for the illustrations

Designed by Gregory Rogers
Printed in Hong Kong
Production by Vantage Graphics, Sydney, Australia.

PART OF THE ROYALTIES AND THE PUBLISHER'S INCOME
FROM THIS BOOK GOES TO THE SALVATION ARMY

Way Home

Libby Hathorn

Gregory Rogers

Andersen Press · London

A dog barks and this cat with no name scrambles up a fence.

This boy called Shane sees the little cat and yells,

'Hey, you! Scaredycat!'

The cat with no name hears the loud voice of the boy.
And way up there on the top of the fence, this clever baby
thing rolls itself up. Such a tight little ball of fierce cat.
It growls and then it spits right at the boy called Shane.
Mad as anything!

'Heeey, wild cat! Wildcat!' the boy called Shane laughs,
'Heeey, I like you, Spitfire, Kitten Number One!'
He reaches out slowly, slowly to the ball of spiked fur.
'Sure I do. I like you.
And you like me, don't you?'

The boy called Shane strokes the scared fur.
He talks and talks until growls slide into silence.

'Guess what, Bestcat? You're coming home with me to my place.'
And he lifts the cat with no name from the top of the fence.
He puts it deep inside his zip-up coat.
'Whaddo you reckon, Catlegs?
Shane's taking you home right now.'

Over the bins and garbage bags, past a row of boarded-up houses.
'Yeah — you're with me now, Cat. You'n me, Cat.
And we're going way away home . . .'

But under a pool of streetlights the boy stops.
'Take a look at that Fatcat will you? I'm telling you that cat's
a loser. Eats fancy mince, no kidding. Heaps of it. Right there
at the window. Disgusting. And get that collar. What a joke!'

'C'mon, Mycat, let's shove off.'

The cat with no name is cosy inside the jacket against the heartbeat of the boy called Shane.

'We're going home,' the boy sings. 'You'n me together.'

The cat peers out of the warm boy's warm coat and purrs.

But halfway down the lane the boy stops dead.

'Here's a real nasty sight, Animal! Better belieeeve me. That lot down there, they don't like me.'

'Don't panic now, Catlegs. Act kinda cool. Cool, right. That's us.'

The boy called Shane glances back.

'Uh oh, they're coming. Gotta get out of here. Away from them.'

He pushes the little catface, right down into his jacket.

And he runs hard. But they run hard too.

It's very black down there for the cat in the coat. There's a loud thump and a hard knock and a thud, thud, thud as the boy runs fast. They follow.

Go! Go! Up the lane, all the way they follow. Fast as anything, scared as anything. Go! Get away! Go! To a large lit up street with the people going every which way. Right to an edge of a wide shiny river of cars.

'Hold tight, Kittycat, while I scare this lot.'

The boy leaps out into the road.

There's a blare of horns, a screaming of tongues and tyres.

But the cat with no name feels safe in the boy's jacket.

'Ahhhh,' the boy called Shane yells as he dives through.

They won't follow him here.

And all the way down the other side of the lit up road the boy
is laughing and laughing. Past a showroom. Six shiny
sports cars, all in a row and one of them raised way up
high on a floor that's turning and turning.

'You can come out now Whiskettes.
No worries. Hey, just take a look.
Vroom vroom. You and me in a Jag. Vroom vroom.
Huh, but they've only got red . . . and we want green.'

Past busy windows and clean steps. Past a crumbling dark church. Past the sharp smell of food shops. And the cat in

'Got yourself a cat, Shane?' a girl asks.

'I'm taking it home to my place,' he tells her,

'Right now. Non-stop, express!'

'Bye, Shane,' she calls after him.

But the boy called Shane stops again.

'See they cook stuff right on the table in front of you.

Stacks of meat and things.

But don't get ideas, Hungry.

No pets allowed, places like this.'

Past the light-and-stripe of the slatted shop blinds.

Past houses all lit up.

Past a thin forlorn park.

The boy called Shane peers down another long lane.

'No worries, Skinny Minny. Plenty of ways to go home.

But a dark shape comes bounding out of the long lane.
And the cat with no name sees a flash of cruel teeth,
hears the angry loud bark of the monster dog,
smells the blood and the hunger and danger.

Quick, in a panic, out of the coat, onto the fence, and into the
tree. Then up and up and up. The cat scritches and scratches
to the topmost, thinnest branches. It's hanging high in the
night city sky.

'Hey, Upcat — where you gone to, stupid?'
The boy called Shane, hand over hand, goes up and up
towards the topmost, thinnest branches.

'Forgot to tell you, Blackeyes, there's milk for you at home.
Lots and lots. So come here, okay?
We're friends. You said so.
C'mon, pussycat.'

A steady brown hand reaches out. 'I'd break my neck for you.
You know that? I'd break my stupid neck . . .'

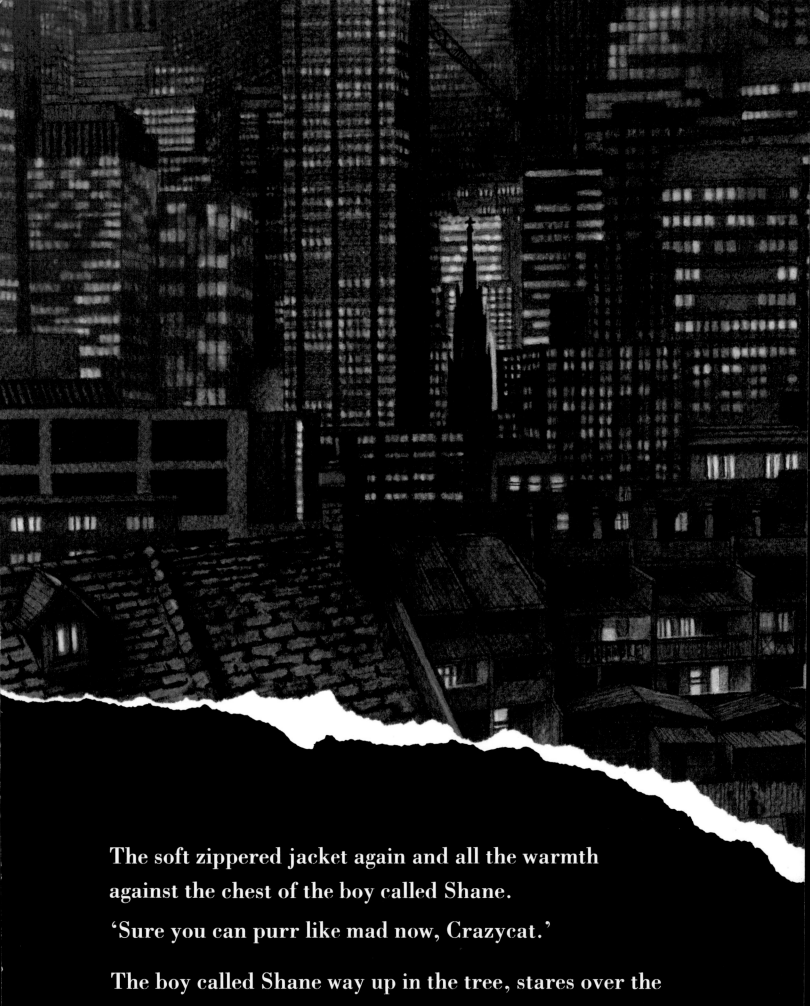

The soft zippered jacket again and all the warmth
against the chest of the boy called Shane.

'Sure you can purr like mad now, Crazycat.'

The boy called Shane way up in the tree, stares over the
streets and lanes. Across the rise and fall of the big sea
of city below.

'Get that stack of big buildings.

Nobody lives in them — no way.

They're all mostly empty — specially nights.

I've been there once.

They're to look at I guess.

So why don't you look, Kittycat?

Hey, get those people down there.

Talk about crazy.

There's our Jag too.

It's cool up here, I reckon.'

'Guess what? I can see our place, Catseyes.

And we gotta go down right now.'

Hand over hand, branch over branch, down the slippery trunk
to the tindery fence. It's an easy jump to the ground.

The boy called Shane takes the cat with no name back down.

'No more pussyfooting, Cat Number One. This time, we're
going right on home.'

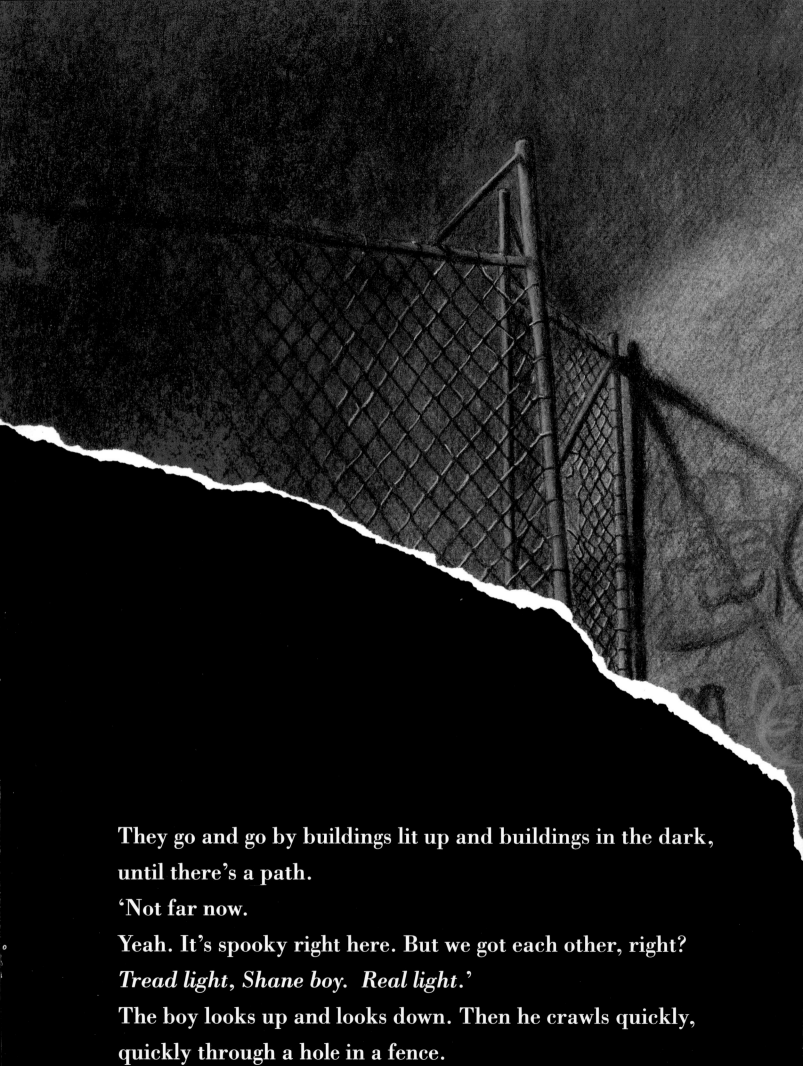

They go and go by buildings lit up and buildings in the dark,
until there's a path.
'Not far now.
Yeah. It's spooky right here. But we got each other, right?
Tread light, Shane boy. Real light.'
The boy looks up and looks down. Then he crawls quickly,
quickly through a hole in a fence.

'From here on it's okay as anything, Noname.
No dogs, I promise. No fights.
And milk like I told you. Heaps of it.
Hang on now, we're nearly home.'

'Down there and round here and we're almost — hey,
hold on real tight a minute,
through here and yes, yes! This is it, Mycat!

This is my place.
Just like I said.
It's okay now.
You're safe.'

'Here we are.
We're home!'